To _____ Diana

From _____ Mom ♡

Other books by Gregory E. Lang:

WHY A DAUGHTER NEEDS A DAD

WHY A SON NEEDS A MOM

WHY A SON NEEDS A DAD

WHY I LOVE GRANDMA

WHY I LOVE GRANDPA

WHY I CHOSE YOU

WHY I LOVE YOU

WHY MY HEART STILL SKIPS A BEAT

WHY I NEED YOU

WHY WE ARE A FAMILY

WHY WE ARE FRIENDS

GOOD LUCK, GRADUATE

BROTHERS AND SISTERS

SIMPLE ACTS

LOVE SIGNS

LIFE MAPS

THANK YOU, MOM

THANK YOU, DAD

BECAUSE YOU ARE MY DAUGHTER

BECAUSE YOU ARE MY SON

WHY A

Daughter

NEEDS A

Mom

Gregory E. Lang

100 REASONS

CUMBERLAND HOUSE

Published by Cumberland House, an imprint of Sourcebooks, Inc.
P.O. Box 4410, Naperville, Illinois 60567–4410
(630) 961–3900 Fax: (630) 961–2168
www.sourcebooks.com

Printed and bound in China
OGP 10 9 8 7 6 5 4 3 2

TO BECKY——THANK YOU

· INTRODUCTION ·

MY DAUGHTER, MEAGAN KATHERINE, and I share a close relationship, albeit one that has changed remarkably since she has matured into a young teenager. Once my constant companion, my playful partner in crime, my most adoring audience, my child has become less enchanted with me as she has entered the initial phases of becoming a woman. Gone are the days of holding hands in public, kissing on the lips, and waking up to find that she had slipped beneath my bedcovers sometime during the night. These treasured gestures of affection are now replaced with brief and discrete touches, small talk, her need for privacy, and the occasional impatient admonishment: "Dad, I am not a little girl anymore."

I struggle with feelings of loss, and at times I cannot resist the impulse to implore my daughter to confide in me, to tell me what thoughts occupy her mind and what feelings beat in her heart. When she doesn't, I hang my head and worry that something has happened to us, convinced that we will never again be as close as we once were. Sometimes I fret that I cannot identify what my child needs or understand why she acts as she does. These thoughts occur to me when I am alone and my judgment is clouded by my sorrow. Thank God for moments of clarity, when I reassure myself that these changes aren't so perplexing after all, that they are, in fact, what should be expected and what should be supported, if indeed I intend for my child to become the strong, independent woman I hope for. It is then that I accept without reluctance that a dad cannot be everything to his daughter. It is then that I see so clearly that she needs her mother, too.

Becky, my ex-wife, and I have been divorced nearly ten years, and we share joint custody of our only child. Meagan lives for a time with me, and then her mom, and back to me. Becky and I live only a few miles apart. We have keys to each other's home, we talk on the telephone often, share meals together now and then, negotiate agreements about enforcing household rules or extending new privileges, resolve disputes about what we might do differently in our relationship with Meagan, and help each other in her care. Long ago we agreed that though we had resigned ourselves to becoming ex-spouses, we would never become ex-parents. It is as parents that our partnership lives on, and it is as parents that we overcome our issues with each other to find a way to do what is best for Meagan. It is in that role, as my partner in parenting, that Becky has been most valuable to me, especially as I learn to accept that my daughter is, most certainly, not a little girl anymore.

As my relationship with Meagan has changed, so too has her relationship with her mother. Now her most trusted confidante, Meagan enjoys lengthy and enthusiastic telephone conversations with her mother, discussing boys, girlfriend spats, celebrity news, or the latest reality television show. Now her fashion consultant, Meagan and her mom shop for hours, get their hair and nails done, and agree that when a girl packs her bags, she must include an abundant selection of shoes, "just in case." Now her preferred safe harbor, Meagan turns to her mother for consolation, protection, and understanding. As a woman, it is Becky who can comprehend what I cannot. As a mom, it is Becky who can give what I cannot. I admit that I occasionally look upon their relationship with a twinge of jealousy, but also always with deep joy and satisfaction that it is what it has become. Their relationship is not only good for them, but for me as well. It is after a late-night telephone call from Becky, explaining to me what I could not see or comforting me about some parental insecurity, that I am thankful she is the mother of my child.

A daughter needs a mom for many reasons, and by the very nature of the differences between men and women, some of these reasons may never be clear to me, but that does not negate their vital importance in a girl's life. Daughters need moms to help them understand what is happening to their bodies, to teach them how to make sound decisions regarding boys, to show them how to care for themselves, how to care for their children, and how to care for their marriage. Daughters need moms because they understand that sometimes tears come for no reason, that bad moods may simply mean nothing at all, that chocolate is a necessity, that being silly is fun, and that everything does not have to be practical or in accordance with a schedule. Daughters need moms because dads cannot be everything for them. Daughters need moms to help them grow into the wonderful women they have the potential of becoming.

I am not a mother, nor am I a daughter, and therefore in the minds of some, perhaps ill-equipped to write this book. However, I am an astute observer of human relationships, and I am a member of a family. My family, comprised of a dad, a mother, and a child, is not unlike many, if not most, other families. It includes laughter and tears, hugs and arguments, surprises and disappointments, giving and taking, sacrifices and rewards. Although she lives in two houses, Meagan still has one family because her mother and I parent her together, love her together, and compromise with each other on her behalf. It is in gratitude to Becky for helping me give Meagan a sense of family that I wrote this book. I hope the story of our family will stir other ex-spouses to rally around their children and embrace the role they share as parents, and in doing so, give their children a more complete family experience, even if in two homes. With this book I hope to give other daughters and moms cause for celebrating what is unique and special about their relationship. I hope, too, to reassure Meagan that I understand, accept, and encourage her as she grows into a woman and reaches beyond me for what she needs. And finally, with this book, I say to Becky, thank you. Thank you for giving me such a wonderful gift, our child. Thank you for being such a great mom, giving to Meagan what I cannot. And thank you for continuing as my partner and giving me friendship when I need it most.

WHY A
Daughter
NEEDS A
Mom

A

Daughter

· *Needs a* ·

MOM

to provide her with memories
that will last forever.

A

Daughter

· *Needs a* ·

MOM

· ·

who is never more than
a phone call away.

· ·

A

Daughter

· *Needs a* ·

MOM

TO ASSURE HER THAT SHE ALWAYS
HAS A PLACE TO COME HOME TO.

....

because no one understands girls
like a mom.

....

TO REMIND HER THAT IN FAITH
THERE IS FELLOWSHIP.

A

Daughter

· *Needs a* ·

MOM

TO SOOTHE THE PAIN OF A BROKEN HEART.

·

to teach her that sometimes choosing to wait is a good idea.

·

TO TEACH HER THAT YOU CANNOT MAKE
SOMEONE LOVE YOU, BUT YOU CAN BE
SOMEONE WHO CAN BE LOVED.

A

Daughter

· Needs a ·

MOM

....

to tell her that beauty never fades
if you look in the right places.

....

A

Daughter

Needs a

MOM

TO TEACH HER HOW TO BE A LADY.

·

*to tell her not to be afraid
to seize the moment.*

·

TO POINT OUT THAT THERE IS
A DIFFERENCE BETWEEN BEING
ADVENTUROUS AND BEING WILD.

A

Daughter

· Needs a ·

MOM

....

who believes it is okay to see things differently.

....

A

Daughter

· *Needs a* ·

MOM

TO TELL HER THAT THE ROAD TO
HAPPINESS IS NOT ALWAYS STRAIGHT.

·

to explain that the sweetest flower
may not always be the prettiest.

·

TO CARRY HER WHEN SHE IS TIRED.

A

Daughter

Needs a

MOM

....

to teach her how to cook.

....

A

Daughter

· *Needs a* ·

MOM

TO TEACH HER THAT CLASS
NEVER GOES OUT OF STYLE.

·

*to teach her to love her friends,
no matter what they do.*

·

TO TEACH HER TO LAUGH AT HERSELF.

·

*to teach her that even true love
requires compromise.*

A
Daughter
· Needs a ·
MOM

....

who knows how to let loose and have fun.

....

A

Daughter

· *Needs a* ·

MOM

TO TELL HER WHAT SHE SHOULD
EXPECT FROM A GOOD MAN.

·

to prepare her for becoming a wife.

·

TO SHOW HER HOW TO RAISE A FAMILY.

A

Daughter

· *Needs a* ·

MOM

....

who can play on her level.

....

A

Daughter

· *Needs a* ·

MOM

··

because there are some things
a dad just can't handle.

··

A

Daughter

· *Needs a* ·

MOM

....

to read to her.

....

A

Daughter

· Needs a ·

MOM

to show her how to give back to others.

A

Daughter

· Needs a ·

MOM

TO SHOW HER HOW
TO FIX HER HAIR.

....

to help her on her wedding day.

....

TO PREPARE HER FOR WHAT SHE WILL
FACE WHEN SHE LEAVES HOME.

A

Daughter

· Needs a ·

MOM

TO SHOW HER HOW TO USE HUMOR
TO LIGHTEN HEAVY LOADS.

·

*to show her how to put a little love
in everything she does.*

·

TO TELL HER NOT TO LET PRIDE GET IN
THE WAY OF FORGIVING SOMEONE.

·

to encourage her to be grateful.

A

Daughter

· *Needs a* ·

MOM

....

to catch her if she falls.

....

A

Daughter

· Needs a ·

MOM

······························

to remind her to be playful,
no matter how old she is.

······························

A

Daughter

· Needs a ·

MOM

....

to remind her, on the bad days,
that she is not alone.

....

A

Daughter

· Needs a ·

MOM

....

to protect her from strangers.

....

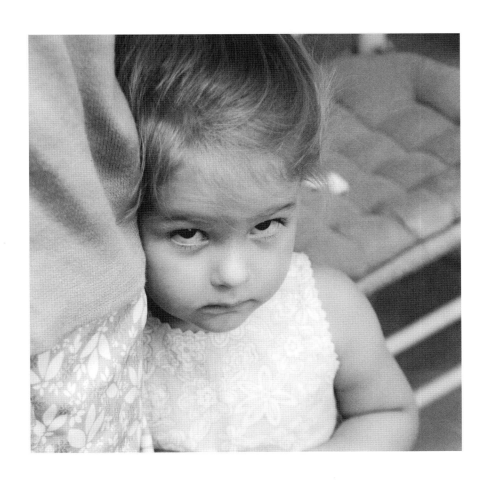

A

Daughter

· Needs a ·

MOM

TO HELP HER LEARN HOW TO
COLOR INSIDE THE LINES.

.

*to show her how to make use
of what she already has.*

.

TO MAKE SURE SHE ALWAYS
RECEIVES MAIL.

.

*to tell her that it is okay
to be a tomboy.*

A Daughter

Needs a

MOM

to remind her to save some time
and energy for herself.

A

Daughter

· *Needs a* ·

MOM

....

to help her choose a prom dress.

....

A

Daughter

· Needs a ·

MOM

who shares with her the
wisdom of generations.

A

Daughter

· *Needs a* ·

MOM

TO SHARE IN HER EXCITEMENT WHEN SHE
FALLS IN LOVE FOR THE FIRST TIME.

·

to share her daydreams with her.

·

WHO WANTS TO HELP MAKE
HER WISHES COME TRUE.

·

to love her for who she is.

A

Daughter

Needs a

MOM

··

to encourage her to be
whatever she wants to be.

··

A

Daughter

Needs a

MOM

to show her how to love someone
with all her heart.

A

Daughter

· Needs a ·

MOM

....

to explain to her how to set limits with boys.

....

A
Daughter
Needs a
MOM

....

to help her see that death is a part of life.

....

A
Daughter
· *Needs a* ·
MOM

TO TEACH HER THAT THE PATH TAKEN
MEANS AS MUCH AS THE DESTINATION.

to teach her that her body is a temple.

TO HELP HER DISTINGUISH THE
DIFFERENCE BETWEEN LOVE AND LUST.

*to remind her that there is a
rainbow after every storm.*

A

Daughter

Needs a

MOM

....

to teach her how to look her best.

....

A

Daughter

Needs a

MOM

....

to teach her not to wait until
tomorrow to say, "I'm sorry."

....

A

Daughter

· *Needs a* ·

MOM

....

to teach her to make thankfulness a habit.

....

A

Daughter

· *Needs a* ·

MOM

to teach her that every tree
takes a while to grow.

A

Daughter

· *Needs a* ·

MOM

....

to encourage her to laugh as often as possible.

....

A

Daughter

· *Needs a* ·

MOM

....

to give her the freedom to express herself.

....

A

Daughter

Needs a

MOM

TO SHOW HER THE COMFORT
OF A WARM EMBRACE.

···

who knows how to put a
smile on her face.

···

TO SING HER TO SLEEP.

A

Daughter

· *Needs a* ·

MOM

....

to listen closely to what troubles her.

....

A

Daughter

Needs a ·

MOM

to teach her that she should know herself
better than anyone else does.

A

Daughter

· Needs a ·

MOM

TO INSTILL PATIENCE IN HER.

·

*who never grows tired
of holding hands.*

·

TO TEACH HER THE
ART OF CONVERSATION.

A

Daughter

· *Needs a* ·

MOM

TO TELL HER THAT GRUDGES ARE
TOO BURDENSOME TO CARRY.

to nurture her imagination.

WHO TELLS HER OF THE SPECIAL PLACE
SHE HOLDS IN HER HEART.

A

Daughter

· Needs a ·

MOM

....

to show her that enthusiasm
for life is contagious.

....

A

Daughter

Needs a

MOM

....

to indulge her individuality.

....

A

Daughter

· *Needs a* ·

MOM

WHO NEVER HESITATES
TO SHOW AFFECTION.

•

*who will sing along with her when her
favorite song comes on the radio.*

•

WHO DOES NOT LOSE HER IDENTITY
IN THE ROLE OF WIFE AND MOTHER.

•

*who shows by example that community
involvement is a worthy pursuit.*

A

Daughter

· Needs a ·

MOM

....

to teach her that she is responsible
for her own happiness.

....

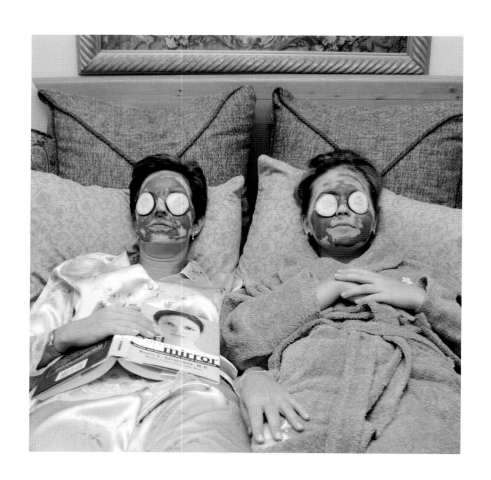

A

Daughter

Needs a

MOM

to remind her that she has the right
to indulge herself now and then.

A
Daughter

• *Needs a* •

MOM

TO MAKE SURE SHE KEEPS
A TRUE HEART.

·

to comfort her through her tears.

·

TO CHALLENGE HER TO STRIVE
FOR WHAT IS JUST BEYOND HER REACH.

A

Daughter

Needs a

MOM

....

who can read the expression on her face.

....

A

Daughter

· *Needs a* ·

MOM

....

to teach her how to care for children.

....

A

Daughter

· *Needs a* ·

MOM

to teach her that you cannot start a life over,
but you can change the way it ends.

A

Daughter

· *Needs a* ·

MOM

....

to teach her to lift her voice in praise.

....

A

Daughter

· *Needs a* ·

MOM

TO HELP HER INTERPRET
THE LANGUAGE OF BOYS.

·

to tell about her first kiss.

·

TO FLASH THE FRONT PORCH LIGHTS
WHEN IT IS TIME TO COME INSIDE.

A

Daughter

· Needs a ·

MOM

to teach her that women
are not bound to the home.

A

Daughter

· Needs a ·

MOM

....

to teach her not to let a good day
slip from her fingers.

....

A

Daughter

· *Needs a* ·

MOM

TO GIVE HER THE COURAGE
TO STAND UP FOR HERSELF.

·

*to teach her that when nothing
seems right, do something normal.*

·

TO REMIND HER TO SAY NICE THINGS
WHEN SHE TALKS TO HERSELF.

A

Daughter

· *Needs a* ·

MOM

....

because without her she will have less
in her life than she deserves.

....